For my children, whose inquisitive minds inspired me to write this book.

For fellow parents, whose years of late-night elf antics have them well-prepared to move on to the next chapter in their holiday traditions.

About this book:

First paperback edition in this format 2021

Copy editing by Tiny Tales Editing
Book layout design by Jodi Giddings

ISBN 978-1-7363520-2-1 (paperback)
ISBN 978-1-7363520-3-8 (hardback)
ISBN 978-1-7363520-4-5 (eBook)

Published by Efficacious Books

AN ELF'S JOURNEY HOME

written by **Kristen Denzer**
illustrated by **Rachel H. Brown**

EFFICACIOUS BOOKS

I await this time of year with such anticipation.
I cannot help but wonder: What is the causation?

So many families across the earth
looking for spectacular elves of worth!

What turn of fates
allowed our connection?
My specialty could have been
trash collection,

or possibly even president by election,
mastering diplomacy skills to perfection.

I could have spent my days
in the North Pole Band

or working with reindeer,
giving Santa a hand.

My woodworking skills
could have been perfected.
"Oh, the toys I could have made!"
I reflected.

For many years, how hard I've worked.
All day and night, no tasks were shirked.

Patiently waiting for Santa to see,
that I'm the ultimate Christmas devotee.

We elves all wanted the prized job of scout,
proving we earned it day in and day out.

I passed night-flight training
and earned my yuletide magic degree.

I memorized the routes
and was ready to be an adoptee.

I remember that day
like it was just two days past.

Oh my! Time has flown by
astronomically fast.

Finally, Santa approached
and said it was my time.

At last, I would be adopted
this wintertime!

I recall nervously waiting
in my bright red holiday box,
so excited yet so scared—
an inescapable paradox.

But then I met your family
and they welcomed me with glee.
After some deliberation,
they exclaimed, "We agree!"

Agree on what? I wondered.
And then you shared the thrilling news:
I had a name, and with it
my magic came—it was no ruse!

That first Christmas was one
of the best we've ever had.
Each year since has touched my heart
and made mc so very glad.

Over the years, I've mastered the fastest North Pole flight route,
and had so much fun in your home, gaining quite a bit of clout.

After reporting in each night, I was free to explore and roam,
partaking in mischief all over your home.

I can always
find the best
hiding place—
that's guaranteed.
Some even suggest
I can creep
around as well
as a centipede.

Making you and your family smile
has been my perpetual goal,
so my antics were always approved
by Rudolph's quality control.

Whether in the
entry or kitchen,
I always put on
quite the show!

I'll never forget you.
Oh, how I've enjoyed this
time watching you grow.

The thunder of your footsteps
would bring my attention to focus.

Then I'd hear your parents call,
"Hey kids! You woke us!"

Those precious moments in the warm light of sunrise
meant I'd soon see the excitement in your eyes.

Then your diligent search would begin; it was almost a race
as you'd get closer and closer to discovering my place.

I've watched you learn incredible things on these quests,
like critical thinking and how to give one's best.

You'd work so hard searching
and at times you wanted to give up.

Then you'd find me, teaching you
perspective and never to let up.

Being a part of your holiday joy
has been so special to me.
But I need to be honest now,
if you will allow me to be.

During other seasons, I'm quite lonely
but I continue reporting in.
Never staying with you year-round
leaves me in quite the tailspin.

Moving each season,
never having a permanent abode,
reinforces my longing to stay
and have a consistent zip code.

You always exclaim with such jubilant glee
the very second you lay your eyes on me.

How special and loved that always makes me feel.
That's how I know your home is my ideal!

This past year I have thought quite a bit,
and the time has come, I must admit.

You no longer need your actions reported,
a premise your kindness leaves unsupported.

You've never belonged on the list for the naughty;
evidence that any child does has been spotty.

Besides, coal in a stocking? Come on, puh-lease.
All of us elves know that's just a tease.

It's important you know it's okay to make mistakes;
even adults do in life's game of give and take.

When we make those mistakes, it's essential that we learn
to do what's right—and never reach the point of no return.

No child on earth is totally good or bad;
each one deserves joy and the chance to be glad.

Recently my fellow scouts have shared with me
some much-needed perspective to help me see.

All I've ever wanted was to bring Christmas cheer,
but I realize now that I have instilled some fear.

Some children consider me to be a spy,
not a friend, an idea I must decry.

My purpose has always
been to share
that you're
very special
and how much
you truly care.

Christmas is about joy, mystery, love, and surprise.
It's about wonders, which I think you now realize.
I've seen you embody what Christmas is all about,
and that is why it's time to Santa I reached out.

To Santa I made
the most paramount request,
asking pretty please
to make this the best Christmas yet.

That is why this year is so special,
at least I hope it will be.
It is the year that your Christmas
toy will hopefully be me.

Scout elf adoption is forever; I hope to never again leave.
You are my family. Please keep me so I no longer grieve.

I know some think I relish the life of a goldfish—only watched,
never touched—but that is not my greatest wish.

I want to be with you
in the spring, summer, and fall,
to share smiles and hugs,
not behind an invisible wall.

I know I'm ready,
but are you? We'll see.

Now my final plea:
May I plant my roots
here forever, like a tree?

I am ready.
My quest is complete.
To your life,
I want a front-row seat.

I'm waiting
and wondering.
Are you ready too?
Is it your hope
that I'll be
forever with you?

If you're not ready yet,
I will wait faithfully.
This choice, after all,
can't be made hastefully.

If your answer is
a resounding, "Yes,"
don't worry, it's quite
a simple process.

Please come close,
no need to be shy.
Now I am ready
to no longer fly.

To confirm requires more than a bump or a prod.
Your enthusiastic hug is the lightning rod.

Your hug starts a new chapter; we're together year-round.
I can't wait to try things like the merry-go-around!

Come find me and give me the first hug of many.
Just don't be bashful, because I'd love twenty!

To Santa, I already
shared my goodbyes.
The last step's
up to you to finalize.

Then I will leave
you nevermore.
So, friend, what are
you waiting for?

Made in the USA
Columbia, SC
30 September 2021